Adventures

through the NORTH FORK

Autumn

Written and Illustrated by

Danielle Malmet Rodger

ISBN: 978-1-58776-952-8
Manufactured in the United States of America

NetPublications, Inc.

HUDSON
HOUSE

For *Lea* and *Jamie*

... *my little adventurers*

Anyone who has ever taken an adventure through
the North Fork can always spy a tractor busy at
work. See if you can find the tractor that has been
hidden for you in each picture.

Traveling through the North Fork

       there are so many wonderful things to see...

             Come along on an adventure with me!

The grassy farms all around

With long l o n g paths

to the silver bay

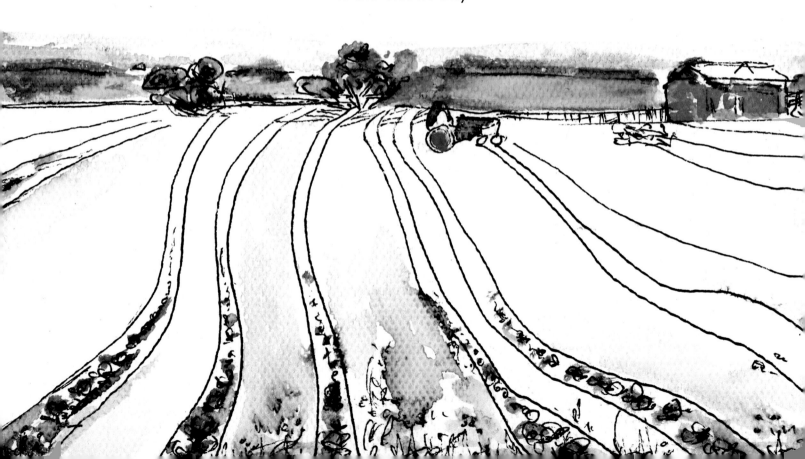

And rows of traveling cornfields

GLITTER gold today

Have you seen...

Pumpkin patch of **haunted** orange

Their

polka-dotted

lawns hide treasures

Apple trees **red** ripe delicious

Caramel covered

indulging pleasures

Have you noticed...

Purple vines dressed in white

Their *ghostly* costumes under the moon

Black birds s w a r m the skies

Their last dance,

happy to leave soon

Look closely…

Crowds of families packed in cars

 CORN HUSKED roof tops

chowder for the road

The setting sun races below the sound

Pink skies lead to their abode

The land is still, quiet and black

Faint yellow lights for the animals in the barns

Crickets sing their lovely lullabies

Goodnight

to the North Fork farms

About the Author

I am a mother of two and have lived on the North Fork of Long Island for 10 years now. It has been a wonderful experience writing and illustrating this book. Please look for my other books as we take more adventures through the beautiful seasons.

If you are interested in purchasing any prints please contact me at daniellemrodger@gmail.com.

You can also find more of my artwork at DanielleMalmetRodger.com.

Thank you to Scott Enstine and Lisa Krekeler for making the pictures come alive and thank you to Blake Dowling and Michelle Lerner for helping me find the words. Thank you to my family always.